MW00888075

Strong Delusion and Lies

Chronicle II of the ABIS

By Britiany A Christian

Ryseville Publishers

A division of Ryseville Ventures

Crete, Nebraska

First edition: January, 2014

All scriptures contained herein are from the Old and New Testaments of

the Authorized King James version of the Bible.

All Photos and Text Copyright © 2014 by Britiany A. Christian

All Rights Reserved

The names of people and many places in this book are fictitious and the invention of the author. Any resemblance to any persons, living or dead, is purely coincidental.

I dedicate this book to
my children,

Joel and Leia.

My love for

them will

never die, but

will continue

for eternity

Britiany A
Christian

SWEET Ü

Also by Britiany A. Christian:

*When I Close My Eyes,
There's Light*

&

*Line of Confusion:
Chronicle I of the ABIS*

Available now on Amazon

Kindle www.amazon.com

Table of Contents

Chapter Six

Chapter Seven

An Invitation

2Thessalonians 2:11

And for this cause God

shall send them strong

delusion, that they should

believe a lie ...

OH BOY!
SAW THAT TITULAR
LINE COMIN!

Prologue

Rose and Abigail walked into the huge airport

There were people everywhere and Rose was more than a little apprehensive. Rose and Abigail were very early and they waited in line as people went through security. Rose fidgeted, as she stood there peering into the crowd, as if she were looking for someone. Suddenly she started hollering,

"Yoo hoo Joshua We're over here!"

Abigail, startled, looked in the direction that Rose was hollering. She watched as Joshua made his way over to them. He looked nervous as he reached over and hugged Rose's shoulder.

"How are you girls?" He asked as if trying to calm

himself. He stared at Abby and she looked down as her

cheeks flushed red.

"Oh we're fine Joshua. Thank you for coming to see

MAM, HE'S NOT GOING

us off." Rose replied with a big smile on her face.

"The airport sure is busy," said Joshua as he looked

around at the crowd, "I'm amazed at all these people

getting ready to go somewhere."

"Actually," Rose smiled wide, "It's pretty exciting

for me. I've never been on a plane before. This will be my

first time and I'm more than a little frightened. I have to

admit though that I'm really looking forward to going to

Israel and then on to Babylon."

There was a pregnant silence as they stood there. Finally
Joshua spoke to Abigail.

"How are you Abby? It's been a while since I've seen you. You look wonderful." He looked into her beautiful blue green eyes and his heart skipped a beat.

"Oh I'm doing fine Joshua. I'm really looking forward to this trip. It gives us a chance to get out of town and I think Rose is going to really enjoy it. She's been anxious to set out on the trip ever since you gave us the tickets at Christmas. They were a lovely present. Thank you so much."

She paused a moment and looked up into his warm brown eyes. Her heart was beating fast, but her voice remained calm.

"And how are you Joshua?" She asked quietly.

"I'm doing good Abby; I just came by to give you some information. I have some friends that live in Israel, in Jerusalem actually. They were friends of Gracie and mine when we were in Bible school. They are pastors of a church and living in Israel with their two children. If you

contact them, I know that they will be happy to show you

around. They are wonderful people.

Here are their names and address."

He handed them a piece of paper that was written

on. Suddenly it was their turn to go through security.

Joshua hugged Rose quickly as she started through.

He held his arms open and Abby moved into them as

though it was the most natural thing in the world to do. He

hugged her tightly and whispered in her ear,

"God be with you and Rose. I will be praying for

you. And if you need me, you just call and I'll be there as

soon as I can."

Abby pulled away shakily and nodded her head. As

she got ready to go passed security, she turned to look at

Joshua. Suddenly, she felt like running back into his arms

and letting him kiss her, but she just gave a little wave and

a smile and went on.

Joshua waited, fingering the open airline ticket in

his pocket until they were out of sight. And then, as

though he couldn't make up his mind, he slowly started

walking toward the exit doors of the airport.

I'M GLAD ABIGAIL AND ROSE ARE MORE EXCITED ABOUT THEIR TRIP THAN THEY ARE SCARED ABOUT THE END TIMES.

2nd Thessalonians 2: 2-12

Now we beseech you, brethren, by the coming of our Lord Jesus Christ, and by our

gathering together unto him,

That ye be not soon shaken in mind, or be troubled, neither by spirit, nor by word, nor by letter as from us, as that the day of Christ is at hand. Let no man deceive you by any means: for that day shall not come, except there come a falling away first, and that man of sin be revealed, the son of perdition;

Who opposeth and exalteth himself above all that is called God, or that is worshipped; so that he as God sitteth in the temple of God, shewing himself that he is God. Remember ye not, that, when I was yet with you, I told you these things?And now ye know what withholdeth that he might be revealed in his time. For the mystery of iniquity doth already work: only he who now *letteth will let, until he be taken out of the way.*

And then shall that Wicked be revealed, whom the Lord shall consume with the spirit of his mouth, and shall destroy with the brightness of his coming: Even him, whose coming is after the working of Satan with all power and signs and lying wonders, And with all deceivableness of unrighteousness in them that perish; because they received not the love of the truth, that they might be saved. And for this cause God shall send them strong delusion, that they should believe a lie: That they all might be damned who believed not the truth, but had pleasure in unrighteousness. But we are bound to give thanks always to God for you, brethren beloved of the Lord, because God hath from the beginning chosen you to salvation through sanctification of

the Spirit and belief of the truth.

Whereunto he called you by our gospel, to the obtaining of the glory of our Lord Jesus Christ. Therefore, brethren, stand fast, and hold the traditions which ye have been taught, whether by word, or our epistle. Now our Lord Jesus Christ himself, and God, even our Father, which hath loved us, and hath given us everlasting consolation and good hope through grace,

Comfort your hearts, and establish you in every good word and work.

THE BIBLE IS SO BORING

Chapter One

Beautiful Israel

Abigail and Rose settled into their comfortable seats for their long trip to Israel. It was first class accommodations and they were thrilled. The trip was non-stop, so they were happy with the nice seats to rest during the trip.

"Oh we are blessed Abby" said Rose, "This is going to be a most comfortable trip. Joshua is a saint for doing this for us. I'm a little frightened though but first class makes it so much easier to bear."

The stewardess stood at the front and gave her instructions. Rose listened carefully so as not to forget the instructions if anything happened. Abigail could see that Rose was getting tense and reassured her by taking her hand.

Then they were off. Rose's stomach jumped as the plane went in the air. She had her eyes closed tightly and held onto Abigail's hand. It seemed as though they were climbing forever but then slowly the plane leveled out. The captain came on the intercom introducing himself, giving the weather, the altitude they were flying, and the time of arrival in Israel. He explained they would be landing in Tel Aviv in 13 hours and Tel Aviv was 6424 miles away. The girls
planned on staying the night in Tel Aviv since it would be so early in the morning, and then on to Jerusalem.

Rose was so excited she was beside herself. The stewardess came by with a menu and drinks. Rose sipped on her soda and marked her menu and for the first time looked over at Abigail. Abigail's eyes were red as though she had been crying. Rose's heart responded in sympathy.

"Abby, what's wrong?" she asked quietly.

Abigail sniffled and daubed her nose with a handkerchief from her purse.

"I don't know Rose, suddenly I feel really sad."

Rose looked at her and nodded her head.

"You're missing Joshua, come on… admit it… It was wonderful seeing him again. "

Abigail took the bottled water and poured more into the plastic cup she was drinking from, and set it in front of her on the tray.

"It's true…you're right," She admitted. "I didn't realize how much I had missed him until I saw him. I've been trying not to think about him or anything that happened at Christmas. But when I saw him…" Her voice trailed off.

Rose didn't know if she should say what was on her mind, but she launched ahead boldly, as was her way.

"Abigail, I know we've talked about this some since John's death. But why would you not want to marry a wonderful man like Joshua. It's obvious that you both care for one another. It's as plain as the nose on your face when you look at him. And the look on his face… oh my…he adores you. I know he loves you so very much. He told me so."

Abigail looked at her startled.

"He did? When did he say that to you?"

"Abby, at Christmas, we sat out on the swing and he told me…he loves you. He fell in love with you the moment he saw you at the hardware store. The man is crazy about you!

Why don't you give him and yourself a chance…I think you will both be very happy together. But you are going to have to trust God and believe that a marriage with Joshua is the right thing to do!"

Abby was thoughtful as the stewardess came by and picked up their menus, and told them dinner would be served soon.

"Rose, you know that the reason I won't marry anyone is because I can't have children. Joshua is young, he's only thirty-six, and can have children again. We both know that he would be happier with someone that can fulfill that desire. I won't be able to do that for him."

Big tears started to roll down Abigail's face once more.

"It's a hard cross to bear," she continued, "because I care for Joshua very much. But I want him to be happy. I won't stand in the way of his happiness. He deserves a

woman that can give him a home with children." *HAVE THEY DISCUSSED THIS?*

Rose listened and her heart was filled with sadness.

She wondered if she should say what had been on her

heart for a long time. Yes, she would say it. It had to be

said.

"Abby, have you ever thought that maybe it was

John who couldn't have children? Didn't you say you had

been checked and that the doctor said there was no

reason why you couldn't conceive? It's possible, Abby, that

John lied to you about being all right in that department."

Abigail looked at her with surprise in her beautiful eyes;

and as Rose watched her, she admired how the teal silk

blouse Abby was wearing brought out the blue green of

her eyes. *YES, SHE STILL HAS EYES*

"He said he had tests done and he was fine. I never saw
any reports but I believed him."

Abby sighed with sadness.

Rose plunged ahead.

"Abby, I think John lied to you…or that girl lied to him that he was the father of her child. Maybe he never had any tests and just maybe he believed that woman was telling him the truth. People can be very deceitful. I don't think you should base your happiness and future on something that may not be true." HERE HERE!

Just then the stewardess pushed the cart down the aisle with their dinner, interrupting their conversation. The stewardess set the food trays in front of them.

"Oh my, this looks so good and I'm really hungry." Rose exclaimed softly, as not to be heard by the passengers in the seats across from them. She must have been overheard, because the man closest to them across the aisle, smiled broadly, and raised his drink to her. Rose became flustered as she realized the man was quite handsome. He had a shock of blond hair with touches of grey, and startling blue eyes that seemed to be lingering on her. She looked away quickly as her heart jumped in her chest. What was wrong with her? She didn't think she had ever reacted like that to a man before in her life.

Feeling like a foolish schoolgirl, she concentrated on the prime rib, garlic mashed potatoes and asparagus spears with hollandaise sauce in front of her, so as to quiet her pounding heart. She looked over at the Neptune salad Abby was poking at, and she was really glad she ordered the prime rib. After all, she had to keep up her strength for this long adventure.

She and Abby finished their dinner, and the stewardess took away the trays. She looked out the window and caught sight of the sunset in the clouds over the water. She pointed it out for Abby to see. They both watched the beauty of God's water coloring of oranges, pinks and purples in the clouds, as the sun sank into the darkening skies and water.

Rose marveled and thanked the Lord with all her heart and soul that she and Abigail were traveling at this fantastic speed headed for Israel. Suddenly, happiness and peace like she never felt before filled her, and in her spirit she knew this was God's plan for her and Abby; and all her misgivings about the storm and the loss of their parents' beautiful home disappeared into the fading light. As she sat there basking in the love of God, she wondered what wonderful surprises lay ahead in Israel for her and Abigail. And with a smile of peace on her face, she closed her eyes and fell instantly asleep.

Chapter Two

We're finally here!

Rose woke as Abigail nudged her shoulder.

"Rose, I have to go to the restroom." Rose put her seat up so Abby could have more room to sidle past her. Abby made her way to the restroom and Rose leaned back in her seat quietly enjoying the soft roar of the plane. All she could think about is that they were getting ever closer to their destination. She looked at her wristwatch. Israel was two hours away. She was surprised. She must have slept quite a while.

Just then the man across the way spoke to her,

"I see that the plane ride doesn't bother you. You looked so at peace while you were sleeping, I envy you." The man said with a faint accent that sounded Russian. He lifted his cup to her.

"I can't fly without a couple of drinks to soothe my nerves. I hate flying." He said with a sigh. "I wish I could have your peace. You looked as though you were smiling when you were sleeping."

Rose looked over at him and smiled as she answered,

"This is my first plane ride, but I leave it all in the Lord's hands. If He wants me to reach my destination, I will, and that gives me a great deal of peace."

The man's face showed surprise. She watched him, enjoying the freedom to look at his face more closely. She could tell he was older, maybe around her age. The laugh lines around his mouth and eyes gave away that he must

smile a great deal.   (HE'S THE DEVIL)

'He is certainly a very good looking man,' Rose

thought to herself. She looked for a ring on his hand and

couldn't see one.

He watched her quizzically and asked,   ?

"You have never flown before? That is amazing.
Then surely you are Jewish?"

"No, I'm a Christian." She replied softly with a

smile. "I just believe that God is in control of everything. I

just leave my life in His hands and He puts His path in front

of me and I follow

it."

He looked thoughtful as he watched her face.

"And you and the woman are going to Israel, for
what reason?" he asked.

"The woman is my sister and yes, we are going to

Israel because it is something I have wanted to do all my

life. I want to walk where my Savior Jesus walked. I have

longed to be in

Israel for a long time. My soul yearns for it."

"You come from Atlanta right?" The man asked

smiling again, quickly changing the subject.

'I like his smile. It's so sincere.' Rose thought to
herself as she answered him,

"Well, actually, we live a ways from Atlanta. We

live in a small town about 60 miles from there."

"And you? Do you live in Atlanta?" Rose queried,

very curious about this man that was so openly studying

her.

"No actually, I live in Israel. I went to Atlanta to see

my sister and her family. She is married to an American

businessman and they live in Atlanta."

Just then, Abigail came back from the restroom.

Rose decided to go to the restroom herself. And as Abigail

sat down, Rose got up and made her way down the aisle. When Rose came back she saw Abigail and the man having an animate conversation. Suddenly, jealousy stabbed her heart; she had never felt that way before with Abigail and it shocked her.

'I'm certainly acting crazy over a man I barely know', Rose thought, as she chastised herself about her feelings and sat back in her seat. The captain came on the intercom and announced they were descending into Tel Aviv.

'Good,' Rose mused to herself, 'this will be over in a little while and I won't have to see that man again.' She sure was getting silly in her old age.

Soon the plane was descending onto the runway. Abigail took her hand to reassure her, and Rose closed her eyes as the wheels dropped onto the pavement and the plane started braking. They taxied for what seemed forever and then they were parked and the personnel connected the jet way for them to leave the plane.

Rose and Abigail grabbed their carryon items from the overhead above them and walked down the long hallway into the airport. It was so exciting to see all the different people in Ben Gurion Airport from all over the world. They were walking about, all in a hurry, trying to get to their destinations. Rose couldn't believe the diversity of nationalities. Rose wondered about this until she realized that the Jews were coming from all over the world, from many different countries to settle in Israel once again. There were people of different shades of olive complexion, black and white, and many Asiatic people, as well as Arabs with their robes and head dress.

The girls went to pick up their luggage from the carrousel, and Rose jumped when a man's voice spoke into her ear.

"We have to stop meeting like this." Startled she gazed up into the most beautiful piercing blue eyes she had ever seen. It was him.

"I'm sure I don't know what you mean." Rose replied pertly as she felt her cheeks glow red. This only made the man smile broader as he watched her reaction with a knowing look on his face.

"Let me introduce myself. My name is Dr. Mikel Gorbeeva. I am a pediatric surgeon in Jerusalem. Here is my card." Rose read the card which said Mikel was head of a surgical practice in Jerusalem. Mikel continued,

"I enjoyed meeting you and your sister very much. Your sister tells me that you are staying in the same hotel as I am. Do you think you and your sister would like to share a taxi with me and then go to dinner with me this evening?"

Just then Abigail came up to them struggling with both their bags. Mikel rushed over to help her,

"Let me assist." He said with kindness in his voice and eyes.

Rose felt terrible. Abigail was trying to handle both their bags while she was talking to this stranger.

"No, it's alright, I think we can manage" answered Abby with a sweet smile on her face.

"Here you go, Rose." Abby said as she handed her bag to her.
Rose handed her Mikel's card, and Abby read it as Rose grabbed her bag and pulled it along on the wheels.

"I was just asking Rose," Mikel said politely falling in step with them, "if you both would be my guests at dinner tonight. I know an excellent restaurant close to the hotel that I know you both would enjoy." He looked expectantly at Abigail.

Abby looked at Rose,

"Would you like to do that Rose?" Abigail asked as they both looked expectantly at her.

"I...I guess so...yes that would be alright. We can rest up before dinner. Yes, that would be fine."

"Come on then...let's share a taxi to the hotel." Mikel offered again as Rose and Abby both nodded in agreement, and both breathed a sigh of relief. They had been worried about taking a taxi alone in a huge city like Tel Aviv so early in the morning. But God provided, as He always did in everything, a man to escort them to their hotel. Mikel flagged down a taxi and helped the driver put the bags into the trunk. They then squeezed into the taxi.

Mikel was average height but was muscular and well built. The girls got as close together as they could get to give him more room. As they drove, he pointed out different points of interest in the early morning light, in particular the magnificent University structure along the way. The girls loved getting this guided tour from someone

who knew his way around this exotic

city.

It was first light and Rose was getting so sleepy.

They were soon at the hotel and the bellmen helped them

out of the taxi and into the hotel. The hotel was

magnificent. It was new and was marvelously designed.

Both the girls were owing and awing over the beauty of

the architecture, made in very striking marble in beautiful

colors. There were huge vaulted ceilings with murals on

them and the walls. The murals depicted scenes of what

looked like ancient cities of Israel. There were very large

beautiful modern crystal chandeliers hanging from the

ceilings, and luscious carpets that your feet luxuriated in as

you walked.

Mikel watched them both, obviously enjoying their

excitement. Soon they were checked in and headed for

their rooms. Mikel took his leave of them in the elevator at his floor.

"I will see you around seven tonight then, in the lobby. The restaurant is close to the hotel. I think you will like it." He said in his charming accent.

Rose's heart moved in response to it, and then shook off the feeling, disgusted with herself.

'He was certainly very good looking and probably had a girlfriend or a lot of women interested in him, or God forbid even a wife', she thought.

She knew absolutely nothing about him. She sighed and followed Abigail and the bellman into their room. It was absolutely gorgeous. There were beautiful beds with luxurious coverings in soft pastel greens, turned down with a chocolate on their pillows. They were on the twentieth floor and the view was magnificent. She immediately walked over to the window to look out.

"Look Abby, see this beautiful sunrise."

They both stood there admiring the sun coming up over the beautiful city. The sun was shining on the water of the Mediterranean making it look like it was on fire. There were very tall skyscrapers and modern office buildings. Their windows glittered with the pinkish, golden hue in the sunrise.

Rose grabbed Abby's hand and they both bowed their heads and said a prayer of thanksgiving for their safe arrival across the ocean. As they said Amen, Rose turned her head and looked at the older parts of the city. There were mosques, synagogues and older buildings that looked like apartments. There were also homes that looked new and others that looked as if they had been there forever. It made this city so exotic, Middle Eastern and mysterious. Rose almost wished they were going to stay here longer to explore the city but maybe some another time.

Abby sat down on her bed and started typing on her cell phone. Rose was curious until Abby showed her what she found. It was Mikel's web site and there was a photo of Mikel with several other people. The description said he was chief surgeon of a medical practice with several doctors. It then went on to say that he had invented a heart valve procedure that had saved many lives. Rose and Abby were most impressed with what they read and smiled at each other.

Abby then went into the restroom to take a bath. Rose looked at her bed and then hopped onto it. It was beyond comfortable; she lay down, closed her eyes and immediately fell asleep.

Chapter Three

Getting to know you

"Rose, Rose, wake up, it's almost six pm and you have to get ready." Abigail coaxed.

Rose shook the blanket off that was covering her and looked up at Abigail standing over her. What was she dreaming? Mikel was talking to her and trying to tell her something, but she couldn't make out what he was saying. It seemed like a warning. She knew it was something very important but when she woke up she couldn't remember.

After her bath, Rose stood at the closet that Abby had hung their clothes. She looked over at Abby's clothes and wish she was a size four so she could borrow something. But she would have to settle for her size ten clothes and nothing seemed right to her now, all her

clothes seemed dowdy and old looking. She looked at

Abigail with her lovely linen colored dress that had a

matching coat and pretty matching heels. She felt a twinge

of envy that her sister always knew what to wear to make

her look her best.

"Rose, we need to hurry or we will be late."

She turned to look once more in the closet and

pulled her newest dress over her head of mauve and pink

pattern. She had liked it when she bought it but now…

"Oh Rose, you look lovely!" Abigail exclaimed.
"Would you like me to do your hair?"

Rose sat down and let Abby brush her hair out and
style it.
"There," said Abby. "You look beautiful!"

After Abby applied a little makeup to Rose's face,

Rose looked into the mirror and was surprised. She

actually looked almost pretty. Abby fixed her long dark

hair half up and the rest down over one shoulder and Rose

thought it looked attractive. Now she was ready to face

whatever was ahead.

Rose looked into Abby's eyes and they were

glistening. She could tell that Abby was excited about

dinner…and seeing Mikel?

"Do you like him?" Rose asked her sister
tentatively, almost afraid to ask.

"Who dear?"

"Mikel."

"Well, yes dear, he's very nice. Don't you like
him?" Abby queried.

"Well, yes…yes I do. But do you like him more
than Joshua?"

Suddenly Abigail finally understood what Rose was
getting at and started to laugh.

"No Rose, I don't like him in that way. He seems

like a very nice man. I'm glad the Lord put him in our path

to get us to the hotel. God always provides a way for us, doesn't He Rose?

Rose felt happy and relieved as Abby put on her coat and she her jacket as they made their way to the elevator. When they stepped off the elevator Mikel was waiting for them. Rose's heart sighed. Could he be any more handsome? He had a dark suit and a mauve colored dress shirt. His tie was mauve and grey pattern. His blond hair was brushed carefully into place and he was clean shaven, the stubble on his face from the plane gone. She was a little startled that they had both chosen to wear the mauve and grey color scheme in their attire and wondered about it. His eyes roved over her in appraisal, but his eyes were unreadable. She couldn't tell if he approved or not.

"We're going to walk…is that okay?" He asked the girls. "The restaurant is very close and I made reservations. We're going to have to hurry. It's always very busy."

He hurried them out the beautiful gold colored and glass revolving door and took each of their arms to walk quickly. Rose could feel his muscular arms beneath his jacket and a thrill of warmth went through her body.

'My goodness, I can't believe how I'm acting.' Rose thought to herself.

Rose was getting out of breath, and was relieved when he finally said,

"Here we are."

The building was old, as if it had been there for centuries. But the restaurant was modern and lavishly furnished inside, and very crowded with people. Everything that was Middle Eastern exemplified this place; from the Persian rugs on the walls, and the murals similar to the ones in the hotel, to the richly colored stone floors beneath their feet.

The Métier' D showed them to their table. Mikel

ordered the house wine. And when it came, he poured

himself a glass to taste, and quickly drained it.

"Would you girls like some wine, their house wine
is really a good vintage."

"No, Rose answered, "We don't drink. I will take
some tea though and what about you

Abby?" Abby nodded in agreement.

He picked up the menu and scanned it quickly.

"Let me order for you, I know what is good here."

He ordered in Hebrew and the waiter left the table. Mikel

sat back in his chair and relaxed with an almost peaceful

look on his face. "So girls, tell me about you," he said as he

poured himself another glass of wine.

"Well," Rose started, "as I told you before, we're

from a small town in Georgia. We are both widows. We

took care of our parents, after our husbands died, until

they passed away. And this is the first time for us out of the country."

"You are both too young to have lost your husbands." Mikel commented, as he stared at the almost empty glass in his hand. Rose could almost see him debating whether he should pour himself another glass.

"Actually," Abby said, "my husband died in a car accident and Rose's husband had been sick for a long time and finally succumbed to his illness."

"Cancer?" Mikel asked softly,

"Yes, cancer of the liver." Rose replied honestly.

"He must have been very young." Mikel said, almost to himself.

"Yes he was…he was only 37 when he died."

"Ah, I'm 45, very tragic, much too young to die."

Mikel looked into his empty glass and didn't say anything for a minute. He then sat his glass down and looked at Abigail.

"And you Abigail, what do you do?" Mikel asked in his Russian accent that made Rose's heart sigh.

"I was a nurse for many years. I just recently worked in our hospital when the area was devastated by tornadoes.

"Really? Tornadoes? How terrible. What happened?"
She then told him about the event that literally changed their lives. He listened carefully and nodded.

"So, you have a new home to live in? How wonderful. But what brings you to my part of the world."

Abby answered him,

"We're Christians. We've wanted to see Israel for a long time, and we have been reading about the ABIS that they have built in Babylon, and will be traveling there to

see that too. Have you heard of it?"

Rose could see Mikel's jaw visibly tighten and she
wondered fleetingly what that meant.

"Who hasn't heard of it. But why would two

American women want to see some machine having to do

with physics that they have built? I would think there

would be other sites in Babylon more appealing for

women to visit, like the museums or the hanging gardens

or even the theme park."

Abby bristled at his remark.

"We want to see that machine. We think it is a

dangerous experiment. We want to see for ourselves what

they are doing. We think it might be causing all the turmoil

in the earth right now, the tornadoes, earthquakes,

volcano eruptions, tsunamis and cyclones. Why there was

an eruption in Iceland that sent ash into the air over Europe for many days!"

"Ah, I see." Mikel said softly and smiled wryly.

"You realize, of course, that there are many experiments going on all over the world most people don't know about, and I am sure you would consider dangerous. There was even a small machine like the ABIS in your own country before it was shut down. There was talk of funding issues but others said there were earthquakes that disrupted the magnets. Of course the four miles of magnets in your country are nothing compared to what they have in Babylon. They have over a hundred miles of magnets that they have been running at half power. When they are done with their upgrade they will be using all 100 percent of their power."

Mikel pondered for a moment before continuing.

"I've read though, in another experiment there at the same site in your country. They still send beams to an underground shaft in another state looking for dark matter…they call it the 'God Particle'. It is very curious though. They have had terrible tornadoes there too. It was not too far from the town with the machine, and the experiment they are sending beams from. I watched on the news that there were 160 tornadoes that touched down in that area." He paused for a moment and then continued thoughtfully.

"There is also another machine in the Middle East that is working with the same intent in mind, a very large microscope looking for particles. I think all these experiments are working together toward the same goal. "

Abby's curiosity got the best of her and she asked him,

"What goal?"

Mikel thought for a moment as if wondering if he should go on with the subject.

"I think their goal is to find passages through the universe. I have read books concerning this and I think they want to travel the way movies are depicting now. They have begun to realize that space travel for man is very nearly impossible any time soon. So they are set in finding another way to go here and there without spaceships. I think it is very curious indeed. I've read a couple of books on physics that explain how they are hoping to accomplish this." "We believe that too," Abby replied, "and that is why these machines are very dangerous. I think there may be a connection to these machines and what happened in our hometown. I believe they caused the tornadoes that touched down and destroyed our home as well as many other homes. We just want to see for ourselves what is happening in Babylon.

And you are right; they did shut down the machine in our country. But like you said they are still doing experiments there, and there is a possibility of them resuming their experiments with the machine again."

He watched them for a moment and then mused,

"So you are determined and I can't change your mind. Although, if it is as dangerous as all that, why would you want to go there?"

"It's a matter of finding out the truth and warning others about it. Our pastor has told us much about it but has never seen it. We just want to see for ourselves if it is benign or dangerous. We are very aware that the prophecy, Revelation 9 in the New Testament, will be fulfilled but we can still pray." Rose replied quietly.

He watched her intently, studying her openly with amusement in his eyes. He wanted to ask what Revelation

9 said, but he didn't want the conversation to turn into a theological argument. He finally said,

"You do know you won't be able to stop them, no matter who you tell. Some people have tried legally to no avail, but I won't say anything more about it."

"We may not be able to stop the experiment but prayer is powerful when there are many praying together over a matter. Who knows, if there are more people that know about this, all our combined prayers may prevent further loss of life and souls. The Word says we are not fighting with flesh and blood but principalities and power of darkness and spirits with unseen bodies. We have an enemy and his name is Satan. He is using anyone and anything he can to destroy lives and souls with his diabolical promises and lies to become like God. He has been lying to people since the Garden of Eden!" Abby answered emphatically.

Mikel looked at them in surprise that two such beautiful women could have such powerful opinions. And he had to admit what they were saying was making him most uncomfortable. Just then their dinner arrived and he was very relieved. He then changed the subject and began telling the girls about himself over their dinner.

The dinner was excellent. There was first, a wonderful matzo soup, and then a delicious cucumber salad. The entree was perfectly cooked lamb with couscous, exotic herbs and mixed vegetables. He gave them the name of the dish but Rose was unable to pronounce it and they all laughed when she tried.

He then told them that he had just lost his wife of twenty three years, six months prior. She had died from an illness they were never able to diagnosis. He was trying very hard to go on with his life.

"My two children, a boy and a girl, are in the IDF, Israeli Defense Force. They are nineteen year old twins and are both gone from home and stationed on the border by Syria. I worry about them very much because it is very dangerous there. So I throw myself into my work. My practice has been my savior and my work helps me to forget, if even for a few hours."

His face filled with sadness and Rose's heart grew heavy with his sorrow. She guessed that was why he drank so much. But she knew from her own heartbreak with her husband that drinking didn't help anything, it only made things worse. She didn't say anything to him about it though.

When they were finished with dinner, Mikel and Abigail chatted for a little while. Rose listened to both of them express their mutual love of the medical profession, and then they left the restaurant. Mikel took leave of them in the elevator at his floor.

"I will be leaving very early in the morning. You have my card if you ever need anything…please call me anytime. I will help you in any way that I can."

And then he was gone.

Rose's heart twinge in sadness when she realized she might never see him again, but there was nothing she could do. He seemed to be more interested in Abigail anyway. He watched Abby quite a bit while they were eating. But who could blame him, Abby was so lovely to look at.

Abigail and Rose went into their room and prepared for bed.

"Mikel is a very sad man." Abby mused thoughtfully to Rose. "There is so much heartbreak in his life. I know how hard it is for a physician to see his loved ones die knowing he can do nothing to change the outcome. It's very hard for them because they are healers and want to fix things."

Rose nodded in agreement and Abby could see tears in Rose's eyes.

"Rose would you like to pray for Mikel?"

Rose nodded, afraid to speak for fear she would break into tears.

"Father God," Abby prayed, "please help Mikel through this trial and affliction that he is going through. Please comfort his heart and give him the peace that surpasses all understanding in Jesus Mighty Name. And please take care of his children that are by the Syrian border. Please loose myriads and myriads of angels to protect them and all the soldiers and people in Israel, in Jesus Name. Also, please Lord, take care of Joshua wherever he is and keep him safe. Please let him know how much we care for him in Jesus Mighty Name."

When Rose looked at Abby she had tears on her face. Rose knew the tears were for Joshua and she hugged her little sister. Rose loved her so much. They both grabbed a tissue from the tissue box and dabbed their eyes and smiled at one another.

"I think we will be seeing Mr. Gorbeeva again." Abby murmured thoughtfully. "Did you see the way he was looking at you?"

Rose looked up in surprise.

"No Abby, he was looking at you."

"Only when you were looking at him, I saw his eyes. He likes you Rose."

Rose didn't know what to say but just slipped into bed. Could that be what Mikel was trying to say to her in her dream...that he liked her? She watched the light of the city filtering in through their window and fell asleep.

I REALLY HOPE ROSE DOESN'T DATE THIS BLOND MISOGYNIST

Chapter Four

Surprises and Kiosks

Rose and Abigail were packing their bags, getting ready to leave the hotel. They were going to catch a shuttle to the bus station and they were hurrying. Suddenly, there was a knock on the door. They both looked at each other in surprise, and Rose went to the door and looked out the peephole. She gave a little cry and opened the door. Joshua was standing there looking disheveled and tired.

"Oh my," cried Rose, "It's so good to see you!" She said as she hugged him tightly.

"Abby it's Joshua!" She turned and looked at Abby. Abby's face was pale, and she was frozen in place as if she had seen a ghost. Rose grabbed her jacket as she watched them both warily.

"I'm… I'm going to grab a cup of coffee downstairs…I will be back later!"

She prayed in her heart as she hurried out the door.

"Dear Lord, please help them both…please that they will reconcile in Jesus Mighty Name. Abby loves him so…I just know it Lord."

She got off the elevator and walked around the promenade of the hotel. There were a couple of small clothing shops, restaurants, a coffee shop, and a jewelry store. She stopped in front of the jewelry store, and stared transfixed at a gold pocket knife with what looked like Hebrew writing and pictures engraved on it. She felt compelled to go into the store and buy it even though it was quite expensive. She put it into her handbag and then looked around for somewhere to get coffee and a little breakfast. She saw a small cheerfully decorated coffee shop and went inside.

She was startled when she saw Mikel sitting at a table staring ahead of him gloomily. Rose was unsure whether to go up to him or not. But just as she was deciding, he turned his head and saw her. With a wide smile on his face that made the corner of his eyes crinkle, as if in delight, he jumped to his feet and pulled a chair out for her.

"Please, Please Rose, sit down. How good to see you again. You are looking wonderful this morning."

She sat down a little shakily, a little startled by his compliment. A waiter came up to them and gave them menus. Rose ordered hot tea with lemon and looked through the menu.

Mikel watched her intently. She looked up into his blue eyes and her heart started racing.

'He is so handsome.' she thought to herself. 'I don't think I've ever seen anyone as attractive as he is in my whole life.'

Mikel was staring at her approvingly in her grey tweed slacks and jacket of the same material. She was also wearing a grey silk blouse with a collar that opened at her throat. She had placed on the back of her chair, a grey leather jacket that complimented her outfit, as well as a grey leather purse. He also noticed a whisper of a chain with a small gold cross around her neck. He sat there watching her with a strange look in his eyes and after a few moments he apologized,

> "I'm sorry; it's just that you are so pretty this morning. I like looking at you."
> Rose's heart skipped a beat. He thought she was

pretty. She was so glad that she had color put in her hair at the hairdresser's before they left for Israel, and had kept

her hair loose this morning at Abby's insistence. She did

look different with the color in her hair and when she

wore it down…much younger. She looked into his eyes

and he seemed so sincere. A warm thrill flooded through

her body. Someone actually thought she was pretty.

"I thought you were leaving this morning. She said
quietly.

"I drank too much last night." He replied honestly,

looking ashamed at his admission. I had a bottle of wine in

my room and I drank most of it. I'm afraid the past took

its toll on me last night. I did too much thinking and it

made me very sad. But I also think, subconsciously, I was

hoping to see you again."

He watched her as if to gauge her expression when

he said this. Rose's heart fluttered at his ardent stare with

what looked almost like hunger in his eyes. She thought

she was just imagining that look and lowered her eyes for a moment, and when she looked back into his eyes again, the look was gone.

"Mikel, a friend of ours just flew in from the states and arrived this morning. I'm sure we will be going together to Jerusalem. Would you like to come with us? I don't know what he and Abby plan but I know they wouldn't mind if you join us." Mikel looked surprised and almost jealous.

"A friend of yours or of Abigail's" He asked gruffly.

Rose smiled and answered softly,

"He's a friend to both of us, but mostly to Abby." It pleased her that he was concerned that she might have a boyfriend. He looked relieved and smiled his warmest smile at her.

"When do you think they will be leaving…I have to start work in the morning. I've been gone far too long from my work."

"Let me call and find out."

Rose called Abby's number and explained that Mikel was still here and would join them in going to Jerusalem if time permitted. Abby explained that Joshua had just gone to his room to rest and he had rented a car for them to go later in the afternoon to Jerusalem.

Rose covered the phone and explained to Mikel the plans. He nodded his head in agreement.

"Maybe you would permit me to show you a little of the sites here in Tel Aviv?" He asked Rose.

Rose readily agreed and asked Abby if she wanted to come with her and Mikel. To Mikel's relief, Abby declined and asked her to keep in touch.

"Now, I have you all to myself," He said smiling in that accent that thrilled Rose so, "If only for a few hours…when are we leaving?"

When she told him, he looked at his wristwatch and added,

"Let's eat a little something then we will go."

She ordered buttered toast with jelly. She was afraid to eat a single bite more because she was so nervous. He ordered a toasted bagel with lox and cream cheese that looked really good. He excused himself and called on his cell phone and talked in Hebrew for a few minutes.

He seemed completely satisfied when he hung up.

"So tell me Rose, what work occupies you in the States."

"I was a bookkeeper for a law firm for quite a few years." She began, "When my husband's health worsen, I quit my job and took care of him until he passed away.

Then I moved in with my parents to help Abby take care of them until they passed away. They were quite elderly when they had me, and when Abigail came along eight years later, it was really a surprise.

We had a wonderful childhood. Abby and I grew up very close. I kept an eye on her along with our nanny. I'm afraid I was more like a little mother to her, which she didn't seem to mind at all. We grew up very close to one another. When I married, my mother quit work at my dad's law firm to take care of Abby fulltime."

Mikel was watching her with what seemed much interest in what she was saying so she went on.

"Actually, I've led a very quiet life. My passion is my faith and my church...I just love it. The pastor and congregation are so wonderful and I'm very happy there. And, I love to cook. My hobby is reading cook books and watching the old episodes of Julia Child. I think I would have loved to have been a chef. Abby says I cook quite well and enjoys my culinary testing on her...she's a willing participant, I think." Rose said laughingly, "At least she doesn't complain."

Mikel chuckled at her last remark but then his face grew somber and he asked.

"If you don't mind me asking, why did your husband drink so much?"

Rose was thoughtful as she watched him, as if trying to decide how much she should tell him.

"My husband and I met in high school and dated most of our senior year. We were in love and when he asked me to marry him right out of high school, I agreed, although my parents were against it. He came from the proverbial wrong side of the tracks, I guess you could say. My parents wanted me to go to college. I think my father wanted me to follow in his footsteps...he was a lawyer and quite an excellent one. He practiced for years and knew everyone that was anyone in our town and state. He wanted more for me and was very disappointed when I chose to marry right out of high school. But I was in love and stubborn.

I married Ken and it was hard for us at first. He was very proud and didn't like my parents trying to help us. But then his brother died in a drowning accident, and that's when he changed for the worse. He and his brother were fishing at the time and his brother decided to go swimming and was caught in a rip current. My husband tried to rescue him, getting caught in the same rip current, and almost drowned himself. When his brother went under he couldn't find him. It took a couple of days before they found his brother's body.

Ken was never the same and started to drink and spent most of his time in the bars, and pretty soon he was an alcoholic and couldn't hold a job. My dad had a friend who had a law firm in our town and helped me to get a job there. I worked and went to school at night. I got my degree and became their bookkeeper. And well, I guess that is that...the story of my life."

Mikel looked sad as he watched her.

"So you have had much pain in your life too." He reached over and put his hand over hers and squeezed it. Rose's heart skipped a beat it was beating so fast. Just then the waiter came with their food and they ate quickly not speaking. When they finished, Mikel paid the bill and they walked back out into the lobby.

"Come, I have a surprise for you."

Mikel walked to the front desk of the hotel and spoke to the clerk there. The clerk handed him some keys and Mikel grabbed her hand and walked her outside. By the curb, was a gorgeous silver luxury car. The bellman opened the car door and helped her inside. Mikel walked to the other side and got into the driver's seat. Rose was

thrilled as she sank into the soft, silver-colored, leather

seats. She put her seat belt on and admired the

dashboard. It almost looked like a plane with all the

buttons and gauges. She had a simple car at home that

was a few years old. Abby had a nicer one but it also was a

few years old. This car was brand new and simply

breathtaking.

"You haven't seen the Mediterranean Sea have
you?" He enquired.

Rose shook her head no and watched the scenery

flying by her car window. All she could think was what a

lovely and modern city Tel Aviv was. Mikel chatted to her

about the different sites they were passing but soon she

could see the water of the Mediterranean. The blue of the

water was extraordinary; the scene of water, sky and

beach looked almost like a painting. Mikel turned onto a beach area and pulled the car into a parking lot.

As she gazed at the sea, it was so picturesque it made her catch her breath. The sea was gently lapping against the shore, the waves softly rolling in. The sky was an intense blue with a few fluffy clouds. There were people all around, in and out of the water, and walking the beach and promenade. The day was warm which she thought was surprising for March. Mikel grabbed her hand and they walked to the shore. Rose crouched down and put her hand in the water. It was surprisingly not that bad, not as cold like one would think for late March.

"Oh Mikel, this is lovely!" She exclaimed, "Thank you so much for bringing me here. I love it."

She looked out at the sea that seemed to go on into infinity. This place was so beautiful almost spiritual.

The Mediterranean…she was finally getting to see it up close for the first time.

Mikel watched her delight and she turned toward him with her eyes shining. A breeze had come up and was gently blowing her long hair onto her face. He took his finger and pulled the strands off her face; and then as if it was the most natural thing in the world, he cupped her face in both his hands and kissed her. Time seemed to stand still for Rose. She never remembered feeling this way in her life…not ever with Ken. She had cared for Ken but not like this. She didn't want this moment to end.

Mikel suddenly pulled away from her and apologized.

"I'm sorry Rose, you don't know me. I don't want you to think that I am taking advantage of you. You are such a beautiful and sweet woman. I couldn't help myself."

KEN PROBABLY WASN'T EVIL

Rose didn't say anything but turned to look out at

the water. She was afraid to speak for fear she would

break into tears. She was afraid she was dreaming and

would wake up and find out none of this was real. He was

so perfect. Was she falling in love with Mikel? She hardly

knew him...how could this be?

Mikel took her hand and they walked the beach

and went up the stairs to the promenade and strolled to

the shops and peered through the windows. Rose was

delighted.

"Mikel, there's a necklace I'd like to get for Abigail. Do
you think we could go in?"

They went into the store and she also saw a little

picture frame that was made out of the rockets that had

been fired on Israel and she wanted to get it for Joshua. It

had the scripture quote, 'With God Nothing Is Impossible'

inscribed on it, and she bought it and the necklace for

Abigail. She put her purchases into her purse and remembered her purchase earlier; the pocket knife.

Mikel took her to one of the Kiosks that were set up on the promenade and bought them both a potato latkes, a traditional Jewish food. As they sat on a bench, Rose exclaimed over the goodness of the treat. They sat in comfortable silence looking out over the sparkling aqua blue water as they ate.

"Where do you come from originally?" Rose asked suddenly.

"Oh, you mean you can tell from my accent I'm not from here?" He teased her.

"Well…well, yes." She sputtered, hoping she hasn't offended him.

"As you probably guessed, I'm from Russia originally. I came from a small town outside of Moscow. When I was twelve we made aliyah to Israel. For the Jew that means to come back home to Israel."

He looked at Rose questioningly and she nodded that she understood.

"It was hard for us at first but my father was good at business and we soon were prospering. I went to college and I met my wife there. She was working on her doctorate in physics and was very intelligent, as well as beautiful. We married right away. She worked at a large American research company in Tel Aviv, when she graduated, to help me stay in medical school. As a matter of fact, she helped develop a product that they now use at the ABIS. She didn't like how the experiment was going at the ABIS when she visited there, and refused to work on anything else having to do with it. Since she was a brilliant physicist, they kept her on; having her work on other projects they were developing. She believed like you and your sister that the experiment was dangerous. She had told me there was much talk among her colleagues about the disasters that were occurring whenever the machine was turned on. And she told me that they were looking to discover things that were not safe for the world. As a matter of fact, there are many who agree with you about the safety of the machine."

Rose was listening intently, looking at him in surprise when he told her that.

"When I was a resident at a hospital, she became pregnant with the twins. They were born and they were the apples of our eye. We loved them both very much and the twins and I are still very close."

He looked moodily out at the water and continued.

"Two years ago she came down with a mysterious illness. She fought valiantly but soon she was very ill. I truly believe it had something to do with the experiment she had worked on for the ABIS. She had said they were using a strange new alloy in the experiment that was extremely unstable and had not been tested for safety."

He paused, almost as though he couldn't go on, but he did.

"I took a leave of absence and took care of her

myself until she passed away. The children and I were

there when she died."

His voice choked up and tears came down his face.

He wiped them away hastily, as if ashamed of them with

the back of his hand. Rose looked into her purse to grab

her handkerchief for him, and saw the pocketknife, and

took it out of her purse. He took her handkerchief and

wiped his eyes with it.

> "May I keep this?" He asked sweetly looking at her
> embroidered initials.
> "Of course." She said happily, as he stuffed the

handkerchief into his pocket. She was impressed that he

wanted to keep something that belonged to her.

OH
MY
GOD.

NO!

"What is that you have there?" He asked as if wanting to change the subject that brought him so much pain.

"Mikel, this is for you." He looked at her in surprise and opened the little sack and brought out the small box.

"What can this be?" He asked as he looked inside. His face broke out into a wide smile that made the corners of his eyes crinkled in delight.

"You know, I looked at this very knife before I went into the café. I have lost my pocketknife and needed a replacement, but this…this is too beautiful for me. I can't accept this…it's much too expensive." He tried to hand it back to her.

"No, Mikel, I bought this for you. I, like you, was hoping to see you again. I was intrigued by it and was wondering what the Hebrew words and pictures meant."

Mikel took it in his big hands and turned it over carefully.

"Actually, it talks about the Israelites deliverance from the Egyptians by Moses and our G-d. See this picture; it is of Moses, as he raised his staff to part the Red Sea to let the children of Israel pass on dry land. And this...this is a picture of the Egyptians cast in the sea when the water went back...it's a remarkable piece to be sure. But I can't accept it though."

Rose took his hand and closed it over the knife.

"I want you to remember me when you look at this knife and know that I am praying for you to my God, and your G-d, the God of Abraham, Isaac, and Jacob, no matter what is happening in your life."

Mikel looked into her eyes and was surprised by the tears he saw in them.

"This woman is so sweet." He thought to himself.

"A woman I can so easily fall in love with."

"All right, I will keep it. I can tell it means a lot to you."

As she nodded her head, suddenly her phone rang in her purse. She answered it and Mikel could tell it was her sister. She talked for a minute and hung up and put the phone back in her purse.

"They are ready to go. Do you think we can go back now?"

Rose was shaking inside as she told him. She didn't want this extraordinary afternoon to end. But they had to get back. Mikel escorted her to the car but before he handed her into her seat he asked,

"What do you think of the car?"

"Mikel, it's beautiful. I love it."

Mikel smiled at her and he got into the car. In no time they were back at the hotel and walking into the lobby. He handed the keys back to the clerk at the desk and spoke to him briefly. The clerk smiled and nodded in

agreement.

> "I am going upstairs to get my things and I will
> meet you back here in a few minutes."

Mikel told her.

> She nodded and they took the elevator and parted

at his floor. She then went to the door of her room and

knocked on it. Abigail answered looking absolutely radiant.

MIKEL IS GOING TO STAB SOMEONE
WITH THAT KNIFE

Chapter Five

Jerusalem

Rose hugged Abigail and Abby wondered why Rose was shaking.

"Are you alright Rose? Your face is all flushed, are you ill?" Abigail watched Rose in concern.

"No, I'm fine. Just a little tired. It's been an exciting afternoon. Mikel took me to the seashore and we walked on the beach and looked through the shops on the promenade. It was wonderful!"

Rose reached into her purse to distract any attempt by Abby to find out more about her afternoon. She was afraid she might say too much and reveal things she didn't want to share with Abby at the moment. She needed time to think about what happened with Mikel on her own before sharing it with Abby. She pulled out the sack with Abby's necklace and Joshua's frame and showed them to Abby.

"Oh Rose, this is so pretty!" she said as she admired the little seashell encased in gold on a delicate gold chain. She traced the frame with her fingers and marveled how beautiful it was, reading aloud the words on it.

"I know Joshua is going to love this. I know just the place in his living room where it would be perfect." She said softly, almost to herself.

"Please help me put the necklace on." She said excitedly. She looked in the mirror admiring it. "It's lovely Rose…thank you so much!"

"And tell me Abby, what happened after I left."

"Rose I was so shocked to see him…I was overcome by the moment. I think at first he thought I was upset with him coming. But I rushed to him and threw my arms around him and he held me as I cried with happiness in his arms. There were tears in his eyes too when I looked into his face. I tried to tell him how I had been feeling and he put his finger to my lips and told me that we would have plenty of time to talk about it later. He did tell me he had gone home and decided to come to Israel too. He quickly packed a bag and was able to book a much later flight. He then told me he was going to his room to rest and that he would drive us to Jerusalem in the car he rented. We need to hurry though…he's waiting. I did the rest of your packing; all your things are in your bag. We need to get downstairs…he's already called twice to see if you were here yet. I told him about Mikel coming with us. He didn't say much and I couldn't tell if he was upset about it or not."

"Oh dear, I hope he's not upset. Mikel is such a nice man. I do hope they like each other."

"I don't think we have to worry about Joshua, he's a fair and just man. He will be able to see that Mikel is a good man too."

The girls grabbed their bags and went down to the lobby. It was funny to see Joshua on one end of the elevator and Mikel on the other. They both smiled broadly when they saw Rose and Abigail, and rushed to get their bags almost colliding in the process.

"Joshua," Abby said smiling at them, "This is Mikel. Mikel, this is Joshua." The men shook hands and then proceeded to get the bags from Rose and Abby. They all followed Joshua out to the rented car and the men put all their bags in the trunk. Rose and Abigail got into the back seat and the men in the front seat, having agreed that Mikel should drive since he knew the way to Jerusalem. Then they were off. Mikel pointed out different historical sites on the way. The scenery was not unlike the southwestern United States. The only differences were the many trees that were everywhere. Mikel explained that it was very barren when the Jews resettled Israel and they began to plant trees and many other flora as well as vineyards and crops. Everything grew here with their tender care and God's blessings, as well as the drip

systems and irrigation they used to water everything.

Soon they were on the outskirts of Jerusalem. Rose

held her breath knowing they were about to enter the

Holy City where Jesus walked and died. As they entered

the modern part of the city, the girls were impressed by

the many modern buildings and thriving businesses. Rose

asked Abigail,

"Can you smell it?" Rose was thinking about the

scripture that told of the sweet fragrance of Christ.

Abigail responded, with her eyes shining,

"Yes I can! There is a sweetness in the air. I don't

think I've ever smelled anything like that before

anywhere." When she looked at Joshua, he seemed to be

sharing their marvel.

Rose breathed in deeply. She had heard an

evangelist once say that Jerusalem was the center of the

universe as far as God was concerned. As she smelled the sweetness in the air she believed what he said. She was where her Savior preached in the Temple, healed the sick, and shared the Passover with his disciples. He then died a horrible death for the sins of the world on the outskirts of the city. The spotless Lamb of God sacrificed for the world to be saved. She could hardly wait to see the Via Dolorosa, the garden tomb; the garden of Gethsemane, and Golgotha where Jesus was crucified. There was also the Western Wall, the Sea of Galilee and so many other sites she wanted to see.

"Israel," she breathed, "We are finally here."

Mikel stopped the car in front of a beautiful home of white stone, archways and black rod iron gates.

"This is my home." He said so humbly that it made Rose's feelings soar for him. UGH ‗‗

"I was hoping you might come in and have dinner with me. I called my housekeeper and she has made us a meal. Would you honor me by sharing a meal with me in my home?" He asked them.

"Yes we would, right girls?" answered Joshua amiably.

They walked into the home and Rose was awed by the simple beauty of it. The walls were stonewashed white, and the furniture was all in white accented with colorful pillows and throws. The walls were covered with paintings that made vibrant splashes of colors on the walls. There were exotic potted plants everywhere, and many Jewish artifacts that were extraordinary. There was a fireplace on one end of the room of white stone mingled with blue and pink stones, with a fire burning in it due to the fact that the air had cooled in the evening.

Rose walked up to the fireplace mantle to look at the pictures that were placed there. A woman with long dark hair and sparkling blue eyes smiled back at her from many of the pictures. Rose guessed that this was Mikel's wife. He was right, she was very beautiful. She looked at the pictures of the children and they looked very sweet and happy. The girl was extraordinarily beautiful, with blond hair and blue eyes. The boy was very handsome with dark hair and blue eyes. A really gorgeous family, Rose thought to herself. She stopped and looked at a small simple wooden cross placed on the mantle in the middle of the fireplace.

Mikel came up next to her and began to tell her about the cross.

"My younger sister gave it to me. She's a Messianic Jew and is hoping I will convert. I told her I was too old and too Jewish to believe in Jesus as Messiah. But she has made an impact on my children. I think they believe what she has told them and have accepted Jesus as Messiah." He revealed, smiling at Rose.

"She believes in Jesus as Messiah?" Rose asked surprised.

"She went to the States to college and was introduced to Messianic Jews there. I guess there were quite a few there at her school. She attended the Church they went to and became a believer. It was at the church that she met her husband; he also is a Messianic Jew. They have two children and are very happy. She gave me this for a birthday gift and I honor her by displaying it."

He paused and looked at his guests.

"The reason I went to the States this trip, was to see my little niece, to help with her surgery. She had a complicated heart problem and it had to be fixed. Her surgeon and I were able to replace the valve in her heart with a new procedure and she is doing exceptionally well now. I have to admit though; you were talking about the power of prayer. I saw a remarkable outpouring of prayer and love for my niece from their church that was hard to deny. The outcome for such a dire circumstance was amazing!"

Rose looked at him and smiled.
'What an extraordinary and humble man to give God the glory by admitting that prayer was responsible for the positive outcome.' She thought to herself. 'I wonder if he used the procedure he invented, like his website said about him.' She didn't dare say anything for fear it would upset him that they googled him to make sure he was who he said he was.

Just then the housekeeper, Irma, an older woman, came in to tell them that dinner was ready. Mikel introduced her to everyone there and raved about her cooking, which made the blush on her already pink, plump

cheeks turn red. He explained that Irma and her husband

both worked for him. Her husband, Mal, short for Malachi,

was the gardener that tended the well kept grounds. Mikel

escorted them to a lovely dining room, and they sat down

at a table, very modern, set with beautiful china and

crystal glassware. Irma had made a brisket with potato

latkes, and roasted vegetables and herbs sautéed in olive

oil and seasonings, as well as a small salad of different

fresh greens.

"I told Irma how you loved the potato latkes so she made
them especially for you."

Rose was honored and smiled a smile at Mikel that
made him beam. Mikel then asked

Joshua to say a prayer over their food.

"My sister's husband always prays a blessing over
the food."

Joshua surprised them all by saying a blessing in Hebrew and then in English. Mikel was most surprised. "You speak Hebrew?"

"Yes," Joshua explained, "I learned it in college. I have an affinity for languages. I learn different languages very easily. And you, you are from Russia?"

Mikel nodded yes and then Joshua started speaking to him in Russian. Mikel laughed in delight and answered him in Russian. They then carried on a conversation for a few minutes to the surprise of the girls.

"Joshua was just telling me that he had a best friend in college who came from Moscow; and that he learned Russian from him, and he taught his friend better English. This is most unusual and enjoyable. I very rarely get to speak my mother tongue anymore."

They all laughed and continued easy bantering until they were done with dinner. It cheered Rose's heart that

Mikel and Joshua were getting along so well. They then retired to the living room and Irma brought coffee to them there. Mikel pointed out different archeological artifacts that he said were copies of ones that had been found in Israel. He explained that he and his wife participated in a dig one summer in college and they both had been very interested in archeology.

He told them to wait a moment while he went back to his bedroom. He then came running into the room with an Indiana Jones hat that made him look just like the character. He shouted tada and then tried to loudly hum the theme to the movie. As the others and Rose laughed till their sides hurt, she loved that he had a good sense of humor and a flair for drama. Rose thought to herself, with his movie star looks, he could easily have played the lead in that movie. They chatted and joked for a while longer and then Joshua looked at his watch and said,

"We'd better go…I have to get the girls checked into their rooms at the hotel before they give them away. Mikel, this was wonderful, I hope we get to spend some time together while we are here."

"And you, are you staying at the hotel too?" Mikel asked Joshua, looking disappointed as if he didn't want the evening to end.

"I'm staying with friends from college. They have a Christian church here. They are expecting me and I've called them so they wouldn't worry."

Mikel was thoughtful, "If you would like to stay here with me, let me know. I would enjoy the company."

"If things change, I might take you up on that." Joshua replied kindly.

Mikel then went over to Rose before he helped her into the car.

"My dear sweet lady, thank you for the wonderful day. Until we meet again, may the G-d of Abraham, Isaac and Jacob, keep all of you safe."

He then took her small hand in his large one and brushed his lips against her hand. Rose was thrilled and her heart swelled with happiness. She smiled at him and gave a little wave as they drove away. When Mikel waved back, still wearing his Indiana Jones hat, she could see something glint gold in the light from the lamps in the yard. He had the gold pocketknife in his hand as he waved to her, which warmed her heart, and made her smile all the more.

Joshua drove straight to the hotel using the directions Mikel had given them.

When they got to their room, Rose was so tired she went to the bathroom for a bath and then to bed. Joshua was gone when she slipped into bed.

"Joshua wants to see the sights tomorrow. There is a tour bus that leaves at nine; can you be ready by then?"

"Yes, of course," affirmed Rose, as she smiled at Abby, "that would be wonderful."

She then put her head on the pillow and promptly fell asleep, dreaming again of Mikel trying to tell her something, but she couldn't make out what he was saying to her. She woke up a little frightened as she remembered the dream. She couldn't shake the feeling he was trying to warn her… but of what? She fell back asleep and slept fitfully the rest of the night.

Chapter Six

Our Lord walked this way!

Joshua was waiting downstairs when they got off the elevator. They stopped by the café

for a little breakfast, and then went and waited with the others for the bus tour to the Holy

Sites. They were all very excited and Rose talked to a few

of the ladies waiting for the bus as Joshua and Abby held

hands and talked in low whispers to each other. Abby

would ever so often, lean her beautiful blond head against

Joshua's chest and he would put his dark head on hers and

wrap his arms around her. Rose was pleased that they

seemed to be working things out but she wished she could

hear what they were saying. Maybe Abby would tell her

later on when they were back in their room. She was so happy that the two people she loved most in the world were finally getting close to… maybe a wedding? Rose's heart was singing. This trip was turning out to be such a big blessing!

'Thank you Jesus!' she whispered in her heart.

And then, there was Mikel, but she wouldn't think about that now. She would keep that tucked away in her heart until she was alone to think. But, she couldn't stop the memory of his lips on hers. She could almost taste the sweetness of his kiss. One of the ladies was speaking to her and finally touched her sleeve to get her attention.

"I say, it's a wonderful day here in Jerusalem." Rose came to herself and answered her,

"Oh, yes…yes it is. It's beautiful today in this amazing land!"

The attractive older woman smiled the prettiest smile at her, but Rose turned away embarrassed that she was carried away by her daydream. Suddenly, her phone

rang and she fished in her purse to retrieve it.

"Hello?" she queried. Mikel's voice boomed out
from the phone.

"Hello, Hello, Can you hear me? My reception isn't
very good. I wanted to see if you and

Abby and Joshua wanted to go out to dinner with me
tonight?"

Rose said she would ask them and call him back in

a moment with the answer. Mikel wanted to spend more

time with her! Her heart was light and her happiness

sublime. Could it be after all these years she might have

someone who truly cared for her. She felt like bursting out

into a song of joy! She kept quiet though, what would

everyone think! Then she imagined everyone in the crowd

singing and dancing with her in joy and couldn't help but

giggle. Abby smiled and looked at her curiously and Rose

smiled back as she asked her,

"Abby, Mikel would like to know if we would like to go to dinner with him tonight."

Abby and Joshua whispered to each other quietly.

Then Joshua reached in his pocket for his phone and made

a phone call.

"Sonia asked if Mikel would like to join us with them for dinner at their home tonight."

Joshua responded.

Rose called Mikel and asked him if he would like to dine with them at Joshua's friends'

home.

"Yes, he would…what time? He said he could pick us up at the hotel."
Joshua spoke into the phone to Sonia.

"She said around 7pm."

She told Mikel and nodded yes to Joshua and Abby

and said goodbye to Mikel. Her heart was surging with joy.

It was amazing to her that a few short days could make

such a difference in her life.

Rose spoke to the Lord in her heart.

'What an awesome place Israel is Lord!

Jerusalem is so wonderful!' Then she took a deep

breath. She could still smell the sweet fragrance of

Jesus in the air, remembering the scripture in 2

Corinthians 2:15-16 KJV: '

>*For we are unto God a sweet savour of*
>
>*Christ, in them that are saved, and in them that*
>
>*perish. To the one we are the savour of death unto*
>
>*death; and to the other the savour of life unto life.*
>
>*And who is sufficient for these things?'*

'Oh, my dearest Lord, how I love thee!' She
whispered to Him in her heart.

Finally, they were on the tour bus and went to the

old part of the city. When they got off the bus, the street

was very crowded with shoppers and what looked like

marketplaces set up everywhere down the Via Dolorosa,

which surprised Rose. She had envisioned a different setting in her mind.

The tour guide tried to be heard above the din of the crowd going about their business. There were tourists, shoppers, Israeli Defense Force soldiers, Arabs, and Jews walking up and down the narrow passages within the high walls of the very old buildings.

The tour guide showed black makers that were round disks up high on the walls that marked the Stations of the Cross. He explained the different stations. The first and the second stations were of Caiaphas the high priest and Pilate trying Jesus. There were three churches that signified these stations, the Church of the Flagellation, the Church of the Condemnation and Imposition of the Cross and the Church of Ecce Homo.

As they walked outside the churches, Rose reached for her Bible in her purse and opened it. She read the verses as they stood there listening to the guide explain the history of these churches. Matthew 26:57-68:

And they that had laid hold on Jesus led him away to Caiaphas the high priest, where the scribes and the elders were assembled. But Peter followed him afar off unto the high priest's palace, and went in, and sat with the servants, to see the end. Now the chief priests, and elders, and all the council, sought false witness against Jesus, to put him to death; But found none: yea, though many false witnesses came, yet found they none. At the last came two false witnesses, And said, "This fellow said, I am able to destroy the temple of God, and to build it in three days." And the high priest arose, and said unto him, "Answerest thou nothing? What is it which these witness against thee?" But Jesus held his peace, And the high priest answered and said unto him, I adjure thee by the living God, that thou tell us whether thou

be the Christ, the Son of God. Jesus saith unto him,

"Thou hast said: nevertheless I say unto you,

Hereafter shall ye see the Son of man sitting on the

right hand of power, and coming in the clouds of

heaven." Then the high priest rent his clothes,

saying, "He hath spoken blasphemy; what further

need have we of witnesses? Behold, now ye have

heard his blasphemy. What think ye?" They

answered and said, "He is guilty of death." Then did

they spit in his face, and buffeted him; and others

smote him with the palms of their hands, Saying,

"Prophesy unto us,

thou Christ, who is he that smote thee?"

Tears sprang into Rose's eyes as she read the

verses of abuse that her Lord was subjected to for our

sakes. And to think she was standing right in the place it happened. Then they were at station two and she read Luke 23:1-25 KJV:

> *And the whole multitude of them arose, and led him unto Pilate. And they began to accuse him, saying, We found this fellow perverting the nation, and forbidding to give tribute to Caesar, saying that he himself is Christ a King. And Pilate asked him, saying, "Art thou the King of the Jews?" And he answered him and said, "Thou sayest it." Then said Pilate to the chief priests and to the people, "I find no fault in this man." And they were the more fierce, saying, "He stirreth up the people, teaching throughout all Jewry, beginning from Galilee to this place." When Pilate heard of Galilee, he asked whether the man were a Galilaean. And as soon as he knew that he belonged unto Herod's jurisdiction,*

he sent him to Herod, who himself also was at Jerusalem at that time. And when Herod saw Jesus, he was exceeding glad: for he was desirous to see him of a long season, because he had heard many things of him; and he hoped to have seen some miracle done by him. Then he questioned with him in many words; but he answered him nothing. And the chief priests and scribes stood and vehemently accused him. And Herod with his men of war set him at nought, and mocked him, and arrayed him in a gorgeous robe, and sent him again to Pilate. And the same day Pilate and Herod were made friends together: for before they were at enmity between themselves. And Pilate, when he had called together the chief priests and the rulers and the people said unto them, "Ye have brought this man unto me, as one that perverteth the people: and, behold, I, having examined him before you, have found no fault in this man touching those things whereof ye accuse him: No, nor yet Herod: for I sent you to him; and, lo, nothing worthy of death is done unto him. I will therefore chastise him, and release him." (For of necessity he must release one unto them at the feast.) And they cried out all at once, saying, "Away with this man, and release unto us Barabbas" (Who for a certain sedition made in the city, and for murder, was cast into prison.) Pilate therefore, willing to release Jesus, spake again to them. But they cried, saying, "Crucify him, crucify him." And he said unto them the third time, "Why, what evil hath he done? I have found no cause of death in him: I will therefore chastise him, and let him go." And they were instant with loud voices, requiring that he might be crucified. And the voices of them and of the chief priests prevailed. And Pilate gave sentence that

it should be as they required. And he released unto

them him that for sedition and murder was cast into

prison, whom they had

desired; but he delivered Jesus to their will.

Rose had read in a popular historian's book, the crowd there shouting these horrible things to Pilate, was actually a group who supported the Pharisees. It was not the general population. They were actually trying to keep the trial very quiet so the crowds in Jerusalem for Passover would not hear of it. The Pharisees feared a riot because Jesus was very popular.

The tour guide led them to the third station. He told them by popular tradition; they say that Jesus fell the first time. Rose knew that this was not in any of the four gospels. She felt in her spirit the reason Jesus did not fall was because of Psalm 91 that says *'the angels will bear you up in their hands lest you dash your foot against a*

stone.'

The devil himself, when he was tempting Christ,

had put him on the top of the pinnacle of the temple,

twisted the scripture, and told him to cast himself down

because the angels would bear him up lest he dashed his

foot against a stone. Matthew 4:3-11:

> *'Then Jesus was led up by the Spirit into the*
>
> *wilderness to be tempted by the devil. And after*
>
> *fasting forty days and forty nights, he was hungry.*
>
> *And the tempter came and said to him, "If you are*
>
> *the Son of God, command these stones to become*
>
> *loaves of bread." But he answered, "It is written,*
>
> *Man shall not live by bread alone, but by every word*
>
> *that comes from the mouth of God."Then the devil*
>
> *took him to the holy city and set him on the pinnacle*
>
> *of the temple and said to him, "If you are the Son of*

God, throw yourself down, for it is written, 'He will

command his angels concerning you, and on their

hands they will bear you up, lest you strike your foot
against a stone'."

> *Jesus said to him, "Again it is written, 'you*

shall not put the Lord your God to the test'." Again,

the devil took Him up on an exceedingly high

mountain, and showed Him all the kingdoms of the

world and their glory. And he said to him, "All these

things I will give you if you will fall down and worship

me," Then Jesus said to him, "Away with you, Satan!

For it is written you shall worship the Lord your God

and him only you shall serve." Then

the devil left him and behold angels came and
ministered to him."

The tour guide told them that the Fourth Station is

not in the canonical gospels, but is a popular tradition of

Jesus meeting His mother on the way to the Cross. It is on

the site of the 19th century Armenian Catholic Oratory and has a carved bas relief that he showed them. They also had many paintings and carvings depicting Mary meeting with Jesus. Rose thought to herself,

'If Mary did indeed see Jesus, it must have been horrifying for her to see her son in that condition.' Rose remembered the scripture, Luke 2:35 KJV:

(Yea a sword shall pierce through thy own soul also,) that the thoughts of many hearts may be revealed.

Rose had read that Jesus had been scourged to the point where He was covered in blood and His flesh hung in ribbons. Rose shuddered at the thought of His mother seeing that and tears welled in her eyes as she grabbed her handkerchief to dab her eyes.

The guide told the group that the church or Oratory was named Our Lady of the Spasm. The fifth station is Simon of Cyrene forced to carry Jesus' Cross. The sixth station is of Veronica wiping the face of Jesus, which is popular tradition and not a tenet of any Christian faith. The seventh station is popular tradition, Jesus falling a second time. And station eight, Jesus meeting the Daughters of Jerusalem. She read in Luke 23:26-31, as tears unashamedly wash down her face:

> *And as they led him away, they laid hold upon one Simon, a Cyrenian, coming out of the country, and on him they laid the cross, that he might bear* it *after Jesus. And there followed him a great company of people, and of women, which also bewailed and lamented him. But Jesus turning unto them said, "Daughters of Jerusalem, weep not for me, but weep for yourselves, and for your children. For, behold, the days are coming, in the which they shall say, Blessed* are *the barren, and the wombs that never bare, and the paps which never gave suck.*

Then shall they begin to say to the mountains, Fall

on us; and to the hills, Cover us. For if they do these

things in a green tree, what shall be done

in the dry?" And there were also two other, malefactors,
                    led with him to be put to death.
"The ninth station is Jesus falling the last time

according to popular tradition," said the tour guide as he

led them toward the Church of the Holy Sepulcher.

"This station is not on the Via Dolorosa and is

located at the entrance to the Ethiopian Orthodox

Monastery and the Coptic Orthodox Monastery of St.

Anthony." explained the tour guide, "Which together form

the roof section of the Chapel of St. Helena in the church

of the Holy Sepulcher."

Before he took them into the Church, he explained

that re-enactments were carried out each Friday by

different groups of people, some professional and some

amateur and were wonderful to watch. Rose hoped she

might be able to see one of these dramas before they left Israel.

When they entered the Holy Sepulcher there was so many people there. They were part of a great crowd but the tour guide kept them together by holding a sign up so they could see where he was going. There were a great many candles in the church. They were in votive cups where many people were lighting them. They were on walls sconces and on candelabras on some of the lower ceilings.

The smell from the candles was overpowering and for a moment Rose was dizzy and thought she might pass out from the great smell of them, but she whispered,

"Jesus help me."

Then she started to feel better. The rest of the ceilings were exceedingly vaulted with intricate carvings on them.

The tour guide stopped with the group in front of murals on the walls depicting Jesus being nailed to the Cross and Jesus hanging on the Cross. He pointed out the place where the Cross reportedly stood and many, of the crowd in the church, were kneeling before it crying and sobbing. The guide showed them the place where they believe Jesus was buried. He explained that there was another place in the city called the Garden Tomb and a hill called Golgotha, but this is where they believed both these places had been. Rose read in her little new testament. Luke 23:33-56:

> *And when they were come to the place, which is call Calvary, there they crucified*
>
> *Him, and the malefactors, one on the right hand, and the other on the left. Then said Jesus, "Father forgive them, for they know not what they do." And they parted His raiment, and cast lots. And the people*

stood beholding. And the rulers also with them derided him, saying, "He saved others; let him save himself, if he be Christ, the chosen of God." And the soldiers also mocked him, coming to him, and offering his vinegar. And saying, "If thou be the king of the Jews, save thyself." And a superscription was written over him, in Greek, and in Latin and Hebrew. THIS IS THE KING OF THE JEWS. And one of the malefactors railed on him, if thou be Christ save thyself and us. But the other answering rebuked him, saying, "Dost not thou fear God, seeing thou are in the same condemnation? And we indeed justly; for we receive the due reward of our deeds: but this man hath done nothing amiss." And he said unto Jesus, "Remember me when thou comest into thy kingdom." And Jesus said unto to him, "Verily, today shalt thou be with me in paradise." And it was about the sixth hour, and there was a darkness over all the

earth until the ninth hour. And the sun was

darkened, and the veil of the temple was rent in the

midst. And when Jesus had cried with a loud voice,

he said, "Father, into thy hands

I commend my spirit." and having said thus, he gave up the

ghost. Now when the centurion saw what was done, he

glorified God, saying, "Certainly this was a righteous man."

And all the people that came together to that sight,

beholding the things which were done, smote their breasts,

and returned. And all his acquaintance, and the women

that followed him from Galilee, stood afar off, beholding

these things. And, behold, there was a man named Joseph,

a counsellor; and he was a good man, and a just (The same

had not consented to the counsel and deed of them;) he

was of Arimathaea, a city of the Jews: who also himself

waited for the kingdom of God. This man went unto Pilate,

and begged the body of Jesus. And he took it down, and

wrapped it in linen, and laid it in a sepulcher that was

hewn in stone, wherein never man before was laid. And

that day was the preparation, and the Sabbath drew on.

And the women also, which came with him from Galilee,

followed after, and beheld the sepulcher, and how his body

was laid. And they returned, and prepared spices and

ointments; and rested the Sabbath day according to the

commandment.

The tour guide stood in front of the place where
they believed that the tomb was located all those years
before. Many people were openly moved and had tears
running down their cheeks. No one even noticed the
crowd milling about them. They were so intent on what
had happened here 2000 years ago as the tour guide
explained the historical facts concerning this place. Rose
continued reading in her Bible. Luke 24 KJV:

Now upon the first day of the week, very early in the morning, they came unto the sepulcher, bringing the spices which they had prepared, and certain others with them. And they found the stone rolled away from the sepulcher. And they entered in, and found not the body of the Lord Jesus. And it came to pass, as they were much perplexed thereabout, behold, two men stood by them in shining garments: And as they were afraid, and bowed down their faces to the earth, they said unto them, "Why seek ye the living among the dead? He is not here, but is risen: remember how he spake unto you when he was yet in Galilee, saying, 'The Son of man must be delivered into the hands of sinful men, and be crucified, and the third day rise again'." And they remembered his words, And returned from the sepulcher, and told all these things unto the eleven, and to all the rest. It was Mary Magdalene and Joanna, and Mary the mother of James, and other women that were with them, which told these things unto the apostles. And their words seemed to them as idle tales, and they believed them not. Then arose Peter, and ran unto the sepulcher; and stooping down, he beheld the linen clothes laid by themselves, and departed, wondering in himself at that which was come to pass. And, behold, two of them went that same day to a village called Emmaus, which was from Jerusalem about threescore furlongs. And they talked together of all these things which had happened. And it came to pass, that, while they communed together and reasoned, Jesus himself drew near, and went with them. But their eyes were holden that they should not know him. And he said unto them, "What manner of communications are these that ye have one to another, as ye walk, and are sad?" And the one of them, whose name was Cleopas, answering said unto him, "Art thou only a stranger in Jerusalem, and hast not known the things which are come to pass there in these days?" And he said unto them, "What things?" And they said unto him, "Concerning Jesus of Nazareth, which was a prophet mighty in deed and word before God and all the people: And how the chief priests and our rulers delivered him to be condemned to death, and have crucified him.

But we trusted that it had been he which should have redeemed Israel: and beside all this, today is the third day since these things were done. Yea, and certain women also of our company made us astonished, which were early at the sepulchre; And when they found not his body, they came, saying, that they had also seen a vision of angels, which said that he was alive. And certain of them which were with us went to the sepulchre, and found it even so as the women had said: but him they saw not." Then he said unto them, "O fools, and slow of heart to believe all that the prophets have spoken: Ought not Christ to have suffered these things, and to enter into his glory?" And beginning at Moses and all the prophets, he expounded unto them in all the scriptures the things concerning himself. And they drew nigh unto the village, whither they went: and he made as though he would have gone further. But they constrained him, saying, "Abide with us: for it is toward evening, and the day is far spent." And he went in to tarry with them. And it came to pass, as he sat at meat with them, he took bread, and blessed it, and brake, and gave to them. And their eyes were opened, and they knew him; and he vanished out of their sight. And they said one to another, "Did not our heart burn within us, while he talked with us by the way, and while he opened to us the scriptures?" And they rose up the same hour, and returned to Jerusalem, and found the eleven gathered together, and them that were with them, Saying, "The Lord is risen indeed, and hath appeared to Simon." And they told what things were done in the way, and how he was known of them in breaking of bread. And as they thus spake, Jesus himself stood in the midst of them, and saith unto them, "Peace be unto you." But they were terrified and affrighted, and supposed that they had seen a spirit. And he said unto them, "Why are ye troubled? And why do thoughts arise in your hearts? Behold my hands and my feet, that it is I *myself: handle me, and see; for a spirit hath not flesh and bones, as ye see me have." And when he had thus spoken, he shewed them his hands and his feet. And while they yet believed not for joy, and wondered, he said unto them, "Have ye here any meat?" And they gave him a piece of a broiled fish, and of an honeycomb. And he took it, and did eat before them. And he said unto them, "These are the words which I spake unto you, while I was yet with you, that all things must be fulfilled, which were written in the law of Moses, and in the prophets, and in the psalms, concerning me." Then opened he their understanding, that they might understand the scriptures, And said unto them, "Thus it is written, and thus it behooved Christ to suffer, and to rise from the dead the third day: And that repentance and remission of sins should be preached in his name among all nations, beginning at Jerusalem. And ye are witnesses of these things. And, behold, I send the promise of my Father upon you: but tarry ye in the city of Jerusalem, until ye be endued with power from on high."* And he led them out as far as to Bethany, and he lifted up his hands, and blessed them. And it came to pass, while he blessed them, he was parted from them, and carried up into heaven. And they worshipped him, and returned to Jerusalem with great joy: And were continually in the temple, praising and blessing God. Amen.

Rose closed her Bible and watched all that was going on around her with lightness in her heart. This place signified the place where Jesus suffered, died and rose again. The angels had proclaimed,

"He is no longer here! Why look for the living among the dead. He is Risen!"

Rose wiped her eyes with her handkerchief.

Indeed, our Lord Jesus is Risen and alive forevermore. And

we will see Him soon…whether through our own death or

in the Rapture. She then looked around her. She was so

engrossed in all that she had witnessed and read in her

Bible that she had forgotten about Abby and Joshua.

I DID' NOT CARE ABOUT THIS

Chapter Seven

Making plans

Rose searched through the crowd for Abby and Joshua, and finally found them only a

little ways behind her. She went over to Abby and grabbed her hand; she could tell that Abby had been crying too. Abby and Joshua both smiled at her as if to say they understood what she had been feeling.

The tour guide said they were ready to go back to the bus and that there would be another tour tomorrow of the other holy sites in Jerusalem. Rose didn't know if she would be up to that tomorrow. This tour had really been very tiring for her. Abby got in the bus first and Joshua helped Rose up the bus steps. She didn't realize how tired she was until they walked to the bus. She was grateful for

Joshua. He seemed to be able to discern how a person was

feeling.

He was such a good person and Rose loved him very much
as a brother.

On the way back to the hotel, they chatted amiably

about what they would do next. Rose said she was anxious

to go on to Babylon to see the ABIS. Abby and Joshua

talked about whether they should take the excellent

highway that had been built into Babylon and drive

themselves or whether they should fly straight into

Babylon as they had an excellent new airport there. Joshua

suggested they wait a day or two before making up their

minds, and Rose and Abby agreed. When they got back to

the hotel Rose wanted to go straight up to their room to

rest. And when they pressed her to go to lunch, she told

them she would order a sandwich and soup from room

service and take a nap. Abby and Joshua decided to take a walk and look at the shops close by and find a place for lunch.

They held hands and walked down the street looking into windows at all the beautiful things for sale. Abby showed interest in a handbag and Joshua insisted on going in and buying it for her. She was really excited. It was in her favorite color, teal, and by a top notch designer. Abby joked with him that she was going to have to buy a whole new outfit to match the bag. Joshua laughed and kissed her, and told her that could be arranged. Joshua took the package the bag was in and carried it for Abby. He then suggested they stop at a café that was close to the store they had just left. As they waited for lunch, they talked amiably about many subjects including the tour which Abby had really enjoyed.

Suddenly, Joshua's face became somber and he changed the subject.

"Abby, I know I told you we would talk about this sometime. But maybe it's time to discuss why you don't want to marry me."

Abby had a look on her face like a little frightened bird ready to fly away, but Joshua reassured her.

"Abby, if you don't want to discuss it now, we don't have too."

"No…no you're right. We have to discuss this. I just don't know where to start." Abby said with a slight frown on her beautiful face.

"Why don't you just start at the beginning." He assured her gently as he touched her hand.

She then told him everything Rose had told him at Christmas. He listened intently not wanting to miss anything she said. When she came to the part about not being able to have children, he stopped her.

"Abby, do not let your fear of not having children get in the way of our happiness. I love you so very much, if we never have a child that is alright with me. I want to be with you. I want to spend the rest of my life with you, and grow old with you, if the Lord should tarry."

"But you deserve to have children. You are still young…I will not keep you from having a family and happiness." Abby replied as tears threatened to fall from her eyes.

"Abby, I have two children that are in safe keeping in the Lord's arms in heaven. If I never have another child that would be fine with me. The most important question Abby…is…do you love me?" Joshua asked softly.

Abby looked at him and tears once more threatened to fall from her eyes. She grabbed her handkerchief from her purse and dabbed at her eyes. She then looked into his warm brown eyes that held nothing but kindness and love in them and she answered him,

"Joshua, I care about you more than I can ever tell you. You are in my heart. You are the best person I have ever met. You love God with all your being and I couldn't find a better man if
I searched the world over."

"But…do you love me?" Joshua asked patiently.

"Yes, yes…I do love you!" Abby murmured looking steadily into his eyes.

Joshua thought his heart was going to jump out of his chest with happiness. He reached into his jacket pocket and brought out the small velvet box he had offered her at Christmas and opened it. The diamonds on the exquisite ring sparkled and danced with fire in the lights of the restaurant. But Abby did not look at the ring; her attention was totally focused on him.

"Abby, you are the love of my life and I long to share my life with you…will you marry

me?"

As he looked into her beautiful blue green eyes,

time stood still for Joshua. This was one of the most

important moments of his life…and heaven…along with

him held their breath.

***

Rose woke with a start. She was shaking. She was

having that dream again about Mikel, but this time

something was terribly wrong. Mikel was standing there in

her dream trying to warn her. She tried to listen but could

not hear what he said. Suddenly, a horrible black hole

opened up with an apparition standing next to the swirling

abyss. Then the creature turned into a human being and

pushed Mikel in the blackness. Rose could only stand there watching, paralyzed with fear. Rose started screaming the Name of Jesus. She could still hear herself screaming Jesus as she woke up. She was terrified.

Shakily, she walked to the bathroom and poured water into a glass and went back to the bed and sat on the edge of it. She drained the water glass and it soothed her jangled nerves.

She was puzzling over something that she had seen in her dream. Yes, now she remembered. The creature had tuned into a human being who was very familiar. He was a very popular figure on the world scene.

Just then Rose was startled by her cell phone ringing. She reached over for the phone on the nightstand next to the bed. She answered without looking to see who it was. Mikel's voice came over the phone.

"How are you my beautiful lady?"

"Oh Mikel," Rose answered, as her cheeks blushed hot at his words. The terror of the dream evaporated as she listened, comforted by his voice.

"I am doing well and you?"

"It's almost time for me to come and get you. I am so excited about seeing you again. I was wondering if I might be able to come early and speak to you alone for a moment."

Rose smiled at his excitement and wondered at it.

"Well, of course, call me when you come to the hotel and we can meet in the lobby."

"Rose," Mikel said, "I don't know what has happened to me. Ever since I met you, you are all I think about. I can't eat or sleep. I know this may sound crazy but I don't think I can let you go back to America without asking you something. I will call you the minute I get there."

Mikel hung up the phone in his excitement without saying goodbye to her. Rose sat on the edge of her bed and wondered what in the world that was all about? Then she remembered the horrible dream and prayed aloud,

"Lord, thy will be done in my life. I don't know what the dream is about or why You are warning me. But please, Lord, don't let me make any foolish mistakes or do anything out of line with your will. I pray this in Jesus Mighty Name! Amen!"

And she began to get dressed to meet Mikel.

**

Mikel rushed out to his car and hurriedly got in it. His only thought was seeing Rose. He had to see her and talk to her. He was very nearly heartsick with his desire to see her again.

Suddenly, his cell phone rang in his pocket. He answered without looking at it.

"Dr. Gorbeeva." He said in Hebrew.

A heavily accented voice came back at him in Russian.

"So my friend, I finally reach you."

"Yes." Mikel answered in irritation wanting to be done with the conversation so he could leave.

"Everything is in place. We are only waiting for your confirmation so we can go according to plan." The voice came back at him.

"Yes, Yes I know. Something has come up and I have to take care of it before I can do anything else." Mikel told the voice.

"Oh, yes, the pretty American woman you are seeing. Yes, we have been watching you Mikel. I hope this distraction will not keep you from what needs to be done. You have not changed your mind have you?" The man on the other end said harshly.

"No, no…I just need some more time." Mikel stammered, his heart feeling as if it would explode in his chest from the horrible fear that was creeping into his body. They were watching him…and Rose!

"Yes, I will give you a few more days. I will call you soon with the information." The voice said before the phone clicked off.

Mikel sat there for a few moments, his thoughts in disarray. He knew what he had to do. He had to see Rose; her beautiful face appeared in his mind like a lifeline. He must see her again and right away. He started the car and hurriedly pulled away from the curb. He then rushed down the road paying no attention to the car that pulled out after him…and followed.

WHAT IN THE WORLD

TO BE CONTINUED. . .

WHAT IS GOING TO HAPPEN BETWEEN ABBY AND JOSHUA? WILL SHE LET HER FEARS GET IN

THE WAY OF THEIR HAPPINESS OR WILL SHE FLING CAUTION TO THE WIND AND MARRY

JOSHUA… AND ROSE, WHAT IN THE WORLD WAS HER DREAM ABOUT? AND WHAT DID MIKEL'S

URGENT CALL TO HER MEAN? WHAT IS HE GOING TO ASK

HER? AND WHO IS MIKEL'S MYSTERY CALLER AND WHAT

IS THAT ALL ABOUT?

AND WHAT ABOUT BABYLON, WILL THEY GO THERE AND UNRAVEL THE MYSTERY OF THE ABIS?

FIND OUT NEXT TIME IN CHRONICLE III, "STONES OF EMPTINESS", COMING SOON TO KINDLE

ON AMAZON.COM.

An Invitation

Dear Friend,

We have only just met but I feel as close to you as a sister or a mother. What if I was to leave this earth tomorrow...what if I never told you about the One that I love with all my soul. He is the best friend I have ever had. He has never left me even though there were times I acted as if He never existed.

There was a time when all I could think about was finding my one true love. Someone I could depend on to love me forever. I searched and searched throughout my whole life and never found such a being. Maybe he only existed in my mind.

But, in my journey, a friend introduced me to someone. She told me things I never imagined about this Person. She said He would never leave me nor forsake me. It didn't matter to Him that I had done so much wrong in my life. He was ready to wrap His loving arms around me and love me just as I am.

He would help me with all the problems in my life. Problems so big...I didn't know where to begin solving them. However, as we walked together and talked together, He began to show me how to solve these mountainous problems, and He worked in so many ways to make my dreams come true. He showed me things I never had thought of to make my life easier.

The things that stand out in my mind are His kindness, His mercy... and His forgiveness. I thought He was up in the sky somewhere. I had no idea that He was as close as my own heart.

All I had to do was just invite Him in.

Jesus...yes...Jesus...that is His name. His name is said as easily as breathing. It brings peace to a weary heart and joy to a soul that thought she could never feel joy again. Jesus...not a curse word...but a friend, my best friend.

Dear friend, indulge me a little further...who knows if we will ever talk this way again. Jesus, my dear friend, loves you too. He loves you and me both. In fact, He loves the entire world because you see...He's God and He created us. He, His Father, and the Holy Spirit, the triune God created us.

I pray that you will invite Him into your heart. Just say:

Jesus come into my heart. I don't know You but I want to know you. I want to feel love as I have never felt before, and to belong to someone like I have never belonged before. I want to look into

Your warm love-filled eyes in eternity and know

that I belong to You.

Dear Jesus, You died a shameful death on

the cross just for me...as if I was the only person

ever created...so that I could be in heaven with you.

You rose on the third day, and now You sit at the

right hand of the Father.

Dear Lord, forgive my sins, and wash me in

Your most precious Blood shed on the cross for me.

Fill me with Your most Holy Spirit Who will be my

Comforter, my Guide and lead me into all Truth.

Thank you Jesus for saving me in Your most

Precious and Mighty Name.

Now, my dear friend, if you have said this prayer...I

will see you in heaven! If you haven't already, I invite you

to read my story, *When I Close My Eyes, There's Light.* I

hope it will help you in your new walk with Him.

Britiany A. Christian

All four Chronicles on sale at amazon.com, *Line of Confusion Ist Chronicle of the ABIS Strong Delusion and lies 2nd Chronicle of the ABIS Stones of Emptiness 3rd Chronicle of the ABIS Millennial Rain 4th Chronicle of the ABIS*

Made in the USA
Middletown, DE
07 January 2023

18771895R00086